EERIE EXPEDITIONS AROUND THE WORLD

THE GHOSTLY GUIDE TO EDINBURGH CASTLE

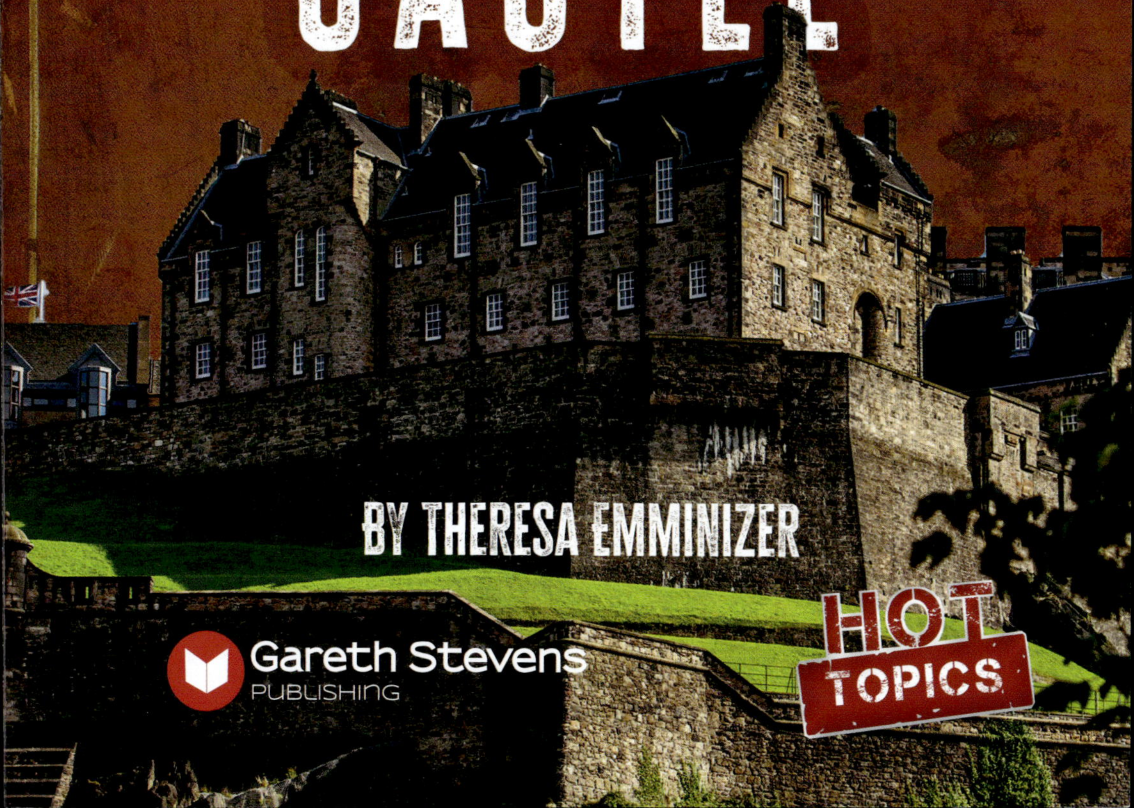

BY THERESA EMMINIZER

Gareth Stevens PUBLISHING

HOT TOPICS

Please visit our website, www.garethstevens.com. For a free color catalog of all our high-quality books, call toll free 1-800-542-2595 or fax 1-877-542-2596.

Library of Congress Cataloging-in-Publication Data
Names: Emminizer, Theresa, author.
Title: The ghostly guide to Edinburgh Castle / Theresa Emminizer.
Description: [Buffalo] : Gareth Stevens Publishing, [2024] | Series: Eerie expeditions around the world | Includes index.
Identifiers: LCCN 2023029130 (print) | LCCN 2023029131 (ebook) | ISBN 9781538291900 (library binding) | ISBN 9781538291894 (paperback) | ISBN 9781538291917 (ebook)
Subjects: LCSH: Haunted castles–Scotland–Juvenile literature. | Edinburgh Castle (Edinburgh, Scotland)–Miscellanea–Juvenile literature. | Ghosts–Scotland–Juvenile literature.
Classification: LCC BF1474 .E46 2024 (print) | LCC BF1474 (ebook) | DDC 133.1/29413/4–dc23/eng/20230707
LC record available at https://lccn.loc.gov/2023029130
LC ebook record available at https://lccn.loc.gov/2023029131

First Edition

Published in 2024 by
Gareth Stevens Publishing
2544 Clinton St
Buffalo, NY 14224

Designer: Tanya Dellaccio Keeney
Editor: Theresa Emminizer

Photo credits: Cover (book texture) normallens/Shutterstock.com; cover (leather strap) donatas1205/Shutterstock.com; cover (Edinburgh Castle) MarcAndreLeTourneux/Shutterstock.com; p.5 agsaz/Shutterstock.com; p. 6 Igal Shkolnik/Shutterstock.com; p. 7 powerofforeveriStock.com; p. 9 ilbusca/iStock.com; p. 10 uncan1890/iStocl.com; p. 11 doublelee/Shutterstock.com; p. 12 Bertl123/Shutterstock.com; p. 13 https://upload.wikimedia.org/wikipedia/commons/a/a4/Edinburgh_valuts_2.jpg; p. 15 matrioshka/Shutterstock.com; p. 17 https://upload.wikimedia.org/wikipedia/commons/1/17/Witches_Well.jpg; p. 19 anastas_styles/Shutterstock.com; p. 21 M.Pakats/Shutterstock.com; pp. 22, 23 Guillaume.B/Shutterstock.com; p. 24 Terriana/iStock.com; p. 25 Dan Jamieson/Shutterstock.com; p. 27 ExFlow/Shutterstock.com; p. 29 Songquan Deng/Shutterstock.com.

Printed in the United States of America

CPSIA compliance information: Batch #CW24GS: For further information contact Gareth Stevens at 1-800-542-2595.

CONTENTS

THE CREEPY CASTLE

Parts of Edinburgh Castle were first built nearly a thousand years ago! Standing atop a volcanic crag called Castle Rock, the castle still overlooks the city of Edinburgh today. With a long, bloody history, this castle is believed to be the most haunted place in Scotland.

SPOOKY STORIES

KINGS, QUEENS, **SAINTS**, AND SOLDIERS WERE BORN, LIVED, AND DIED IN EDINBURGH CASTLE. STORIES OF GHOSTLY MEETINGS AND **PARANORMAL** SIGHTINGS HAVE LONG SURROUNDED IT. SOME DATE BACK HUNDREDS OF YEARS.

WHO HAUNTS THESE HALLS?

Edinburgh Castle changed hands between the British and Scottish many times. It has been the most besieged place in Britain! That means over its history, armies surrounded, attacked, and tried to capture this castle more than any other place in the United Kingdom.

SWORDS IN THE GREAT HALL OF EDINBURGH CASTLE

SPOOKY STORIES

MANY DARK DEEDS TOOK PLACE AT THE CASTLE WHEN POWER CHANGED HANDS. DURING THE BLACK DINNER OF 1440, ADVISORS OF KING JAMES II INVITED THE YOUNG LEADERS OF THE DOUGLAS CLAN TO DINE AT THE CASTLE, THEN KILLED THEM!

THE HEADLESS DRUMMER BOY

Legend has it that a headless drummer boy appears whenever Edinburgh Castle is under attack! He was first sighted in 1650, when castle workers heard the odd sound of a rat-a-tat outside. The next morning, Oliver Cromwell's forces laid siege to the castle.

SPOOKY STORIES

WHAT'S A DRUMMER BOY? IN EARLIER TIMES, DRUMMER BOYS WERE YOUNG BOYS WHO PLAYED DRUMS DURING BATTLES. NOBODY KNOWS FOR SURE WHO THE HEADLESS DRUMMER BOY OF EDINBURGH COULD BE.

THE BAGPIPE BOY

Long ago, a secret tunnel was found leading out of Edinburgh Castle! A young boy was sent down the tunnel with **bagpipes** to find out where it went. Above, people followed the sound of the bagpipe. Suddenly, the playing stopped!

Old English Bagpipe.

SPOOKY STORIES

THE SECRET TUNNEL LIES BENEATH THE ROYAL MILE, A SERIES OF STREETS IN THE HEART OF EDINBURGH. THE ROYAL MILE LEADS DOWN FROM EDINBURGH CASTLE TO THE PALACE OF HOLYROODHOUSE.

THE ROYAL MILE

Others were sent down the tunnel to look for the boy. But he had disappeared! The tunnel was closed, never to be opened again. But sometimes, the sound of bagpipes can still be heard playing from underneath the city streets!

SPOOKY STORIES

VISITORS TO EDINBURGH CAN TAKE UNDERGROUND TOURS! THOUGH THE TUNNEL BENEATH THE ROYAL MILE IS CLOSED, THE EDINBURGH VAULTS ARE OPEN. THESE VAULTS ARE UNDERGROUND STOREROOMS. MANY SAY THEY'RE HAUNTED!

LADY GLAMIS

In 1537, Janet Douglas, also known as Lady Glamis, was burned at the stake outside Edinburgh Castle. Her supposed crime? Witchcraft! People say that the ghost of Lady Glamis can be heard weeping, or crying, and seen walking around Edinburgh Castle.

SPOOKY STORIES

DURING THE 1500s AND 1600s, FEAR OF WITCHCRAFT BECAME A WIDESPREAD PANIC THAT SWEPT ACROSS SCOTLAND. THE SCOTTISH RULER KING JAMES VI SPEARHEADED A PLAN TO HUNT DOWN AND KILL SO-CALLED WITCHES.

Janet Douglas was just one of more than 300 women who were burned as witches on Castlehill, a street outside the castle. The Witches' Well fountain and **plaque** mark the spot where these women lost their lives. Do their ghosts live on at Edinburgh Castle?

SPOOKY STORIES

WOMEN **ACCUSED** OF WITCHCRAFT WERE OFTEN BURNTED ALIVE. THEIR LOVED ONES WERE SOMETIMES **TORTURED** INTO MAKING ACCUSATIONS AGAINST THEM. THERE WERE FIVE MAJOR WITCH HUNTS IN SCOTLAND. THOUSANDS LOST THEIR LIVES.

THIS FOUNTAIN, DESIGNED BY JOHN DUNCAN, R.S.A.
IS NEAR THE SITE ON WHICH MANY WITCHES WERE
BURNED AT THE STAKE. THE WICKED HEAD AND SERENE
HEAD SIGNIFY THAT SOME USED THEIR EXCEPTIONAL
KNOWLEDGE FOR EVIL PURPOSES WHILE OTHERS WERE
MISUNDERSTOOD AND WISHED THEIR KIND NOTHING
BUT GOOD. THE SERPENT HAS THE DUAL SIGNIFICANCE
OF EVIL AND OF WISDOM. THE FOXGLOVE SPRAY FURTHER
EMPHASISES THE DUAL PURPOSE OF MANY COMMON OBJECTS.

THE GHOST DOG

Some say the ghost of Lady Glamis walks with a small, white ghost dog. Others have seen a ghostly black dog running about the grounds. Edinburgh Castle has a small dog cemetery. Perhaps these ghosts are the dogs buried there!

SPOOKY STORIES

MADE IN 1840, THE EDINBURGH CASTLE DOG CEMETERY HAS AROUND 20 HEADSTONES. SOME WERE THE PETS OF SOLDIERS. THE NEWEST HEADSTONE BELONGS TO A DOG NAMED WINKLE WHO DIED IN 1980.

PRISONERS OF WAR

Over the years, many prisoners of war were held at Edinburgh Castle. Some were beaten or tortured. Many died. In 2003, workers began renovating, or fixing, part of the castle called the Queen Anne Tower. Some believe they awoke the prisoners' ghosts!

SPOOKY STORIES

EDINBURGH'S PRISONER GHOSTS WERE MEN HELD IN THE DUNGEONS DURING THE NAPOLEONIC WARS. THESE WARS TOOK PLACE FROM ABOUT 1800 UNTIL 1815. DURING THIS TIME, FRENCH LEADER NAPOLEON AND HIS ALLIES TOOK OVER MOST OF EUROPE.

It's said that ghosts don't like change. As the workers began renovations at the castle, some reported seeing the ghosts of Napoleonic prisoners. They claimed they were being harassed, or bothered, by the ghosts. Some were too frightened to work alone.

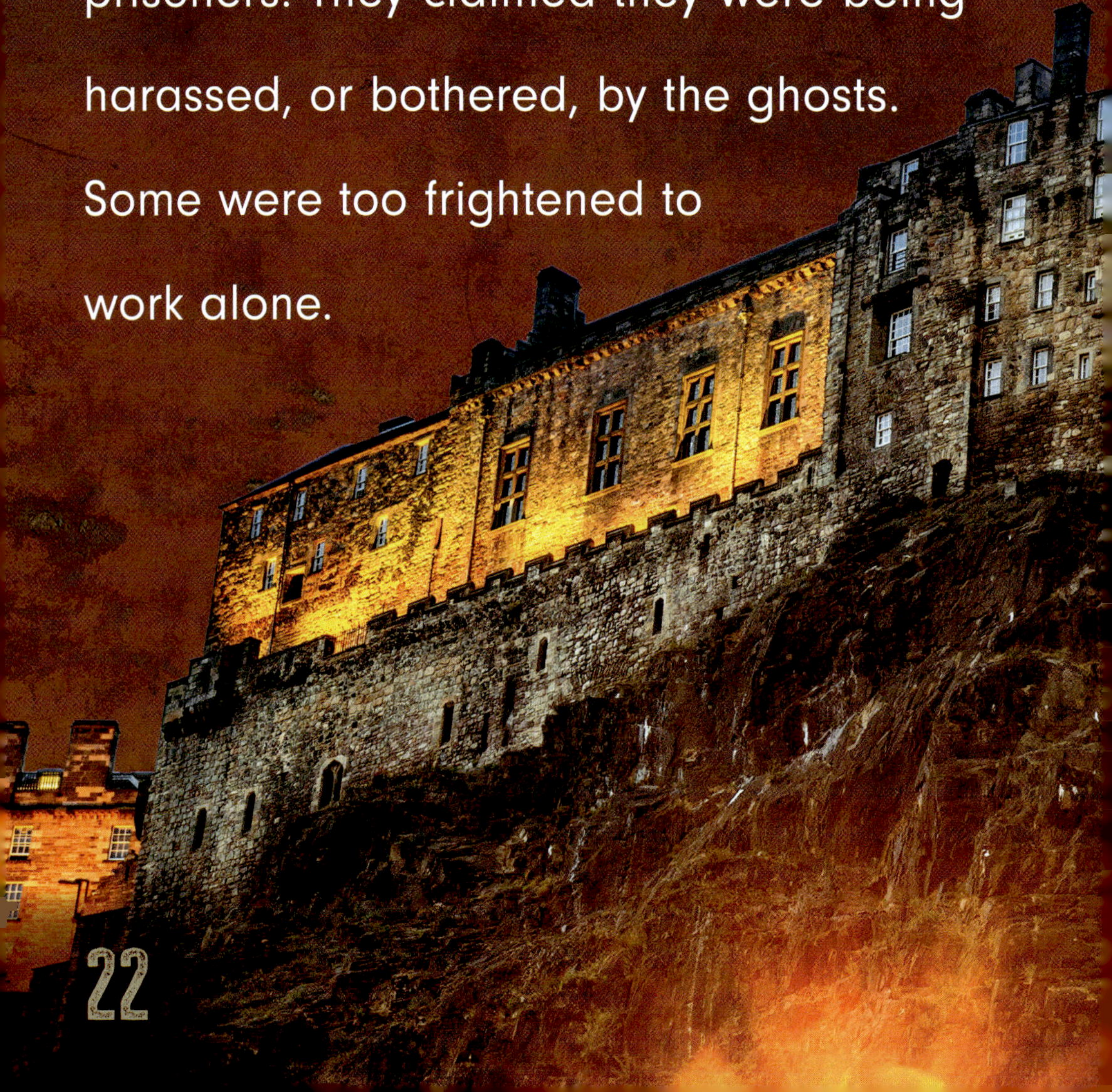

SPOOKY STORIES

THE WORKERS TRIED TO TAKE PICTURES OF THE GHOSTS THEY SAW. THE PICTURES SHOWED BLUE ORBS, OR BALLS, FLOATING ABOVE THE MEN'S HEADS! COULD THEY BE PROOF OF REAL GHOSTS? OR SOMETHING ELSE?

THE DUNG CART GHOST

Do you smell poop? One story says that a prisoner of war tried to get out by hiding in a cart filled with dung, or animal poop! The prisoner hoped to run away once outside the castle walls. Instead, he was thrown off the rocky mountain.

SPOOKY STORIES

PEOPLE WHO CLAIM TO HAVE SEEN THE DUNG CART GHOST SAY HE SMELLS AWFUL. THEY BELIEVE THAT HE TRIES TO THROW VISITORS OFF THE CASTLE WALLS!

THE LEATHER APRON MAN

In 2001, a group of 240 people went to Edinburgh Castle as part of a study of the paranormal. While there, some claimed they felt a burning in their arm. At least one person saw the ghost of a man wearing a leather apron!

SPOOKY STORIES

WHO IS THE MAN IN THE LEATHER APRON? NOBODY KNOWS FOR SURE. EVEN THE VISITORS WHO DIDN'T SEE THE GHOST SAID THEY HAD THE FEELING THAT SOMEBODY WAS WATCHING THEM.

NEMO ME IMPUNE LACESSIT

ASK YOURSELF

Is Edinburgh Castle really haunted? What do you think? Whether or not you believe in ghosts, one thing is for certain: this site has seen many battles, witch burnings, tortures, and deaths. Would you dare to pay it a visit?

SPOOKY STORIES

THERE'S MUCH, MUCH MORE TO KNOW ABOUT EDINBURGH CASTLE! THOUGH THE CASTLE'S GHOST STORIES CAN'T BE COUNTED ON AS TRUTH, THE CASTLE'S FACTUAL HISTORY IS EVERY BIT AS INTERESTING AND CHILLING AS ITS HAUNTED TALES.

HAUNTED HISTORY

600 CE	FIRST WRITTEN REFERENCE TO A FORT BUILT ON CASTLE ROCK.
1093	SAINT MARGARET OF SCOTLAND DIES IN THE CASTLE.
1130–1140	ST. MARGARET'S CHAPEL (THE OLDEST BUILDING ON CASTLE GROUNDS) IS BUILT.
1440	LEADERS OF THE DOUGLAS CLAN ARE KILLED AT THE BLACK DINNER.
1457	A GIANT CANNON CALLED MONS MEG IS PLACED AT THE CASTLE.
1537	JANET DOUGLAS IS BURNED AT THE STAKE.
1650	THE HEADLESS DRUMMER BOY IS SEEN. CROMWELL'S FORCES ATTACK THE CASTLE.
1757–1815	THE CASTLE HOUSES PRISONERS OF WAR TAKEN BY THE BRITISH IN THE SEVEN YEARS' WAR, THE AMERICAN REVOLUTION, AND THE NAPOLEONIC WARS.
2001	VISITORS TO THE CASTLE SAY THEY SEE THE GHOST OF A MAN IN A LEATHER APRON.
2003	WORKERS RENOVATING THE CASTLE CLAIM TO BE HARASSED BY GHOSTS OF PRISONERS OF WAR.

FOR MORE INFORMATION

BOOKS

Croy, Anita. *Ghosts and Poltergeists in History.* New York, NY: Rosen Publishing, 2020.

Morrison, Marie. *Edinburgh Castle Is Haunted!* New York, NY: PowerKids Press, 2021.

WEBSITES

Edinburgh Castle
www.edinburghcastle.scot/plan-your-visit
Learn more about Edinburgh Castle and all there is to see and do there!

Haunted Rooms
www.hauntedrooms.co.uk/edinburgh-castle
Read the stories of the ghosts who haunt Edinburgh Castle.

GLOSSARY

accuse: To blame someone for something.

bagpipe: A musical instrument traditionally used in Scotland.

legend: A story that has been passed down for many years that's unlikely to be true.

paranormal: Not able to be explained by science.

plaque: A flat metal or wood piece that has writing on it used as a way to remember a historic event.

saint: Someone officially recognized for holiness.

torture: To cause someone pain to force them to do or say something.

INDEX